BLUE'S Perfect Picnic Spot

D0150836

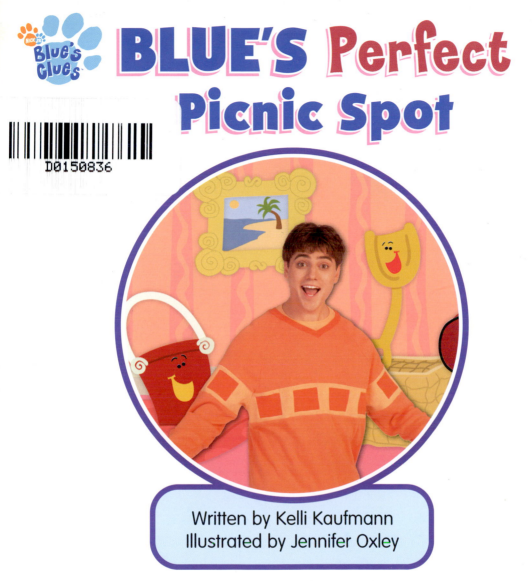

Written by Kelli Kaufmann
Illustrated by Jennifer Oxley

Read along with me, Joe! We're going to play Blue's Clues. Follow along with Blue and me as we pack for a picnic, and look for Blue's Clues along the way! You will know it is time to turn the page when you hear this sound…. Are you ready? Let's go!

publications international, ltd.

Hi! It's me, Joe! It's such a nice, sunny day out, so Blue wants to go on a picnic. Hey, let's play Blue's Clues to find out where Blue wants to have her picnic! Great! Hmm, but where's Blue? Do you see her?

3

Thanks for helping find Blue. Now let's find some things for our picnic basket in the Kitchen. Hello, Mr. Salt, Mrs. Pepper, Paprika, and baby Cinnamon! This is a great picnic basket you're preparing for us.

Let's see, Mrs. Pepper has lined up some silverware. The lineup goes: spoon, fork, spoon, fork. What comes next? Yeah, a spoon! Good job.

Mmm. Those sandwiches look great, Mr. Salt! Do you see a clue? Where do you see a clue? Right! The water! Hey, we have our first clue! We have our first clue! You know what we need? Our Handy Dandy Notebook! Let's draw our first clue.

Blue wants a game to play after the picnic. She wants to play a game that has a ball that you catch with a glove. Hmm. Which of these games has a ball that you catch with a glove? Baseball, yeah! Blue wants to play baseball after our picnic!

It's a sunny day out there! Will you help Blue pick out her biggest hat to keep her head cool at the picnic? Yeah, the sun hat looks like the biggest hat. And let's take Blue's sunglasses, too!

We need a blanket to sit on for our picnic. Let's get it. Oh, do you see a clue? Where? Oh, on the towel. That's our second clue! Let's draw it in our Handy Dandy Notebook.

13

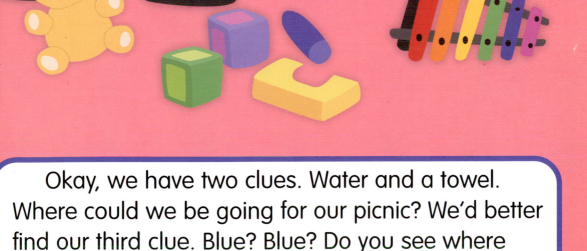

Okay, we have two clues. Water and a towel. Where could we be going for our picnic? We'd better find our third clue. Blue? Blue? Do you see where she's hiding?

Hi, Shovel. Hi, Pail. Are you choosing fruit to take on the picnic? Cool! Blue wants to take a fruit that is round and red. Which fruit is round and red? The apple? Yeah, the apple is round and red!

Hi, Joe! Hi, Blue!

It's picnic time!

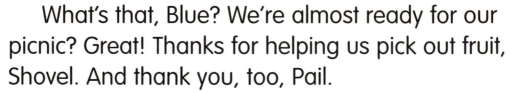

What's that, Blue? We're almost ready for our picnic? Great! Thanks for helping us pick out fruit, Shovel. And thank you, too, Pail.

What? A clue? Where? Oh, I see it. The sand! The sand is our third clue. We have all three clues! That means it's time to sit in our Thinking Chair! Come on!

Okay, let's think. Where could Blue want to have our picnic with water, a towel, and sand? Maybe Blue wants to wrap the towel around her shoulders and fly to the planet of squishy sand for our picnic! No, that's not it. Do you know where Blue wants to go?

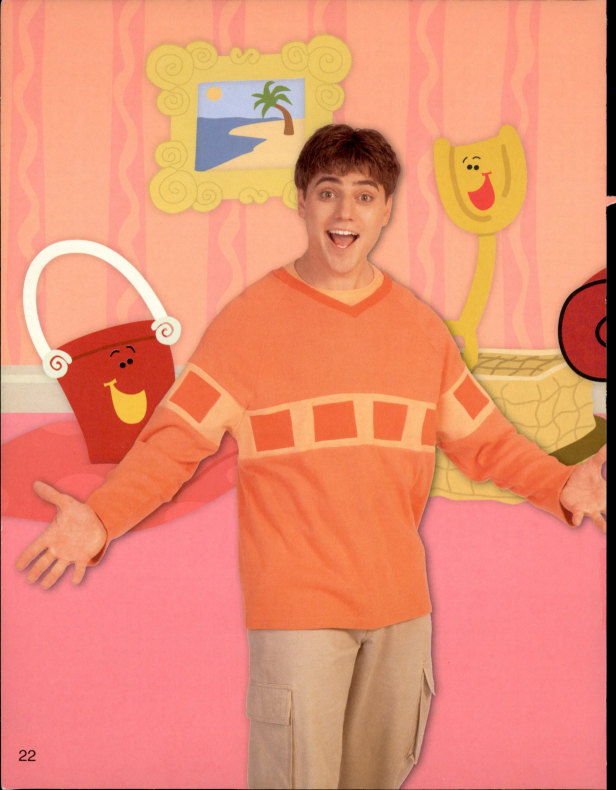

Yeah! Blue wants to go to the beach for our picnic! We just figured out Blue's Clues! We're really smart. Let's all go to the beach for our picnic! I've got the picnic basket. Let's go!

The beach is perfect for a sunny day picnic! And now it's time to eat! Hey, Blue, maybe after we have our picnic, we could throw the baseball around?

Thanks so much for playing Blue's Clues with us. See you next time. Bye!